ABC

LITTLE SIMON
An imprint of Simon & Schuster Children's Publishing Division
1230 Avenue of the Americas, New York, New York 10020
First Little Simon hardcover edition July 2016

For information about special discounts for bulk purchases, please
contact Simon & Schuster Special Sales at 1-866-506-1949 or
business@simonandschuster.com. The Simon & Schuster Speakers
Bureau can bring authors to your live event. For more information
or to book an event contact the Simon & Schuster Speakers Bureau
at 1-866-248-3049 or visit our website at www.simonspeakers.com.
Manufactured in China 0416 SCP
2 4 6 8 10 9 7 5 3 1
Library of Congress Cataloging-in-Publication Data
Olivera, Ramon, author. ABCs on wheels / by Ramon Olivera. —
First edition. pages cm Summary: "A beautifully illustrated, graphic
ABC book featuring all things that go!"—Provided by publisher.
Audience: 3-7. Audience: Pre-school, excluding K.
ISBN 978-1-4814-3244-3 (hc) — ISBN 978-1-4814-3245-0 (eBook)
1. Vehicles—Juvenile literature. 2. English language—Alphabet—
Juvenile literature. 3. Alphabet books—Juvenile literature.
I. Title. TL147.O433 2016 629.04'6—dc23 2015024684

For Mami & Papi

ABCs on Wheels

RAMON OLIVERA

LITTLE SIMON
NEW YORK LONDON TORONTO SYDNEY NEW DELHI

Aa

is for **axle.**

Bb

is for **bumper.**

Cc is for compact.

Dd is for double-decker.

Ee is for empty.

Ff is for full.

Gg

is for **garage**

and **grease.**

MAIL

Hh is for hot rod.

Ii is for ice-cream truck.

Jj is for junkyard.

Kk is for **kaput!**

Ll is for limousine.

Mm is for motorcade.

Nn is for new car.

Oo is for old car.

Pp is for plugged in.

Qq is for **quiet.**

Rr is for **rover.**

Ss is for **stagecoach.**

Tt is for track.

Uu is for underdog.

1
2

Vv is for **victory lane.**

Ww is for **winner.**

Xx is for X marks the spot.

Yy is for yellow cab.

Zz is for zoom!

ABCD
IJKLM
RSTUV

EFGH
NOPQ
WXYZ

→